Ladybird  Readers

Are You Sad, Pablo?

Series Editor: Sorrel Pitts
Text adapted by Hazel Geatches
Song lyrics by Wardour Studios

LADYBIRD BOOKS

UK | USA | Canada | Ireland | Australia
India | New Zealand | South Africa

Ladybird Books is part of the Penguin Random House group of companies
whose addresses can be found at global.penguinrandomhouse.com.
www.penguin.co.uk   www.puffin.co.uk   www.ladybird.co.uk

Text adapted from *Pablo's Feelings* by Andrew Brenner and Sumita Majumdar,
first published by Ladybird Books Ltd, 2020
Based on the *Pablo* TV series created by Gráinne Mc Guinness
This Ladybird Readers edition published 2021
001

PAPER OWL FILMS

Printed in China

A CIP catalogue record for this book is available from the British Library

ISBN: 978–0–241–47554–6

All correspondence to:
Ladybird Books
Penguin Random House Children's
One Embassy Gardens, 8 Viaduct Gardens, London SW11 7BW

MIX
Paper from
responsible sources
FSC® C018179

Are You Sad, Pablo?

Based on
the Pablo TV series

Picture words

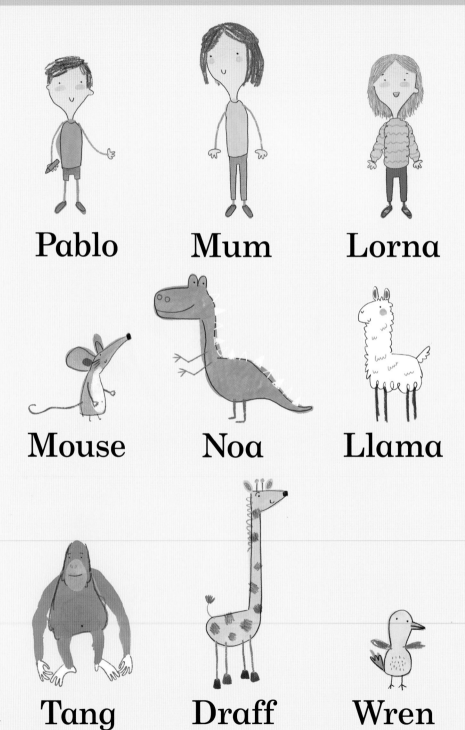

Pablo

Mum

Lorna

Mouse

Noa

Llama

Tang

Draff

Wren

think

mirror

laugh

Pablo and Mum are at home.

"Can you play with Lorna today?" asks Mum.

Pablo thinks, "Yes!", but he does not say it.

Mum phones Lorna.
"Sorry, Pablo cannot
play today," says Mum.

Pablo does not understand.

"Are you sad, Pablo?"
asks Mouse.

"No," says Pablo.

"Are you sad, Pablo?"
asks Noa.

"Are you sad, Pablo?"
asks Llama.

"No," says Pablo.

Mouse draws Pablo.

"Look," says Mouse.
"Your face is sad."

"Look in the mirror," says Mouse.

"In the mirror, my face is sad," says Pablo, "but I'm not sad!"

"Is Pablo sad?" asks Tang.

"No," says Noa, "but his face is sad."

"Look," says Tang. "I'm happy, and my face is happy!"

Pablo laughs!

Pablo looks in the mirror.

His face is sad again.

17

Pablo puts a book in front
of his face.

"Now, you cannot see my sad face," says Pablo.

"I like playing with Lorna.
How can I tell Mum?"
asks Pablo.

21

"Tell her with words," says Draff.

"I cannot find my words," thinks Pablo.

"I can tell Mum with a picture!" thinks Pablo.

Pablo draws a picture.

"You *can* play with Lorna!"
says Mum.

"Yes!" thinks Pablo.

Now, Pablo is playing
with Lorna.

His face is not happy . . .
but Pablo is happy.

Lorna is happy, too.

Activities

The key below describes the skills practiced in each activity.

 Spelling and writing

📖 Reading

💬 Speaking

🎧 Listening*

❓ Critical thinking

🎵 Singing*

✅ Preparation for the Cambridge Young Learners exams

*To complete these activities, listen to the audio downloads available at **www.ladybirdeducation.co.uk**

1 Match the words to the pictures.

1 Mouse

2 Noa

3 Tang

4 Mum

5 Lorna

6 Pablo

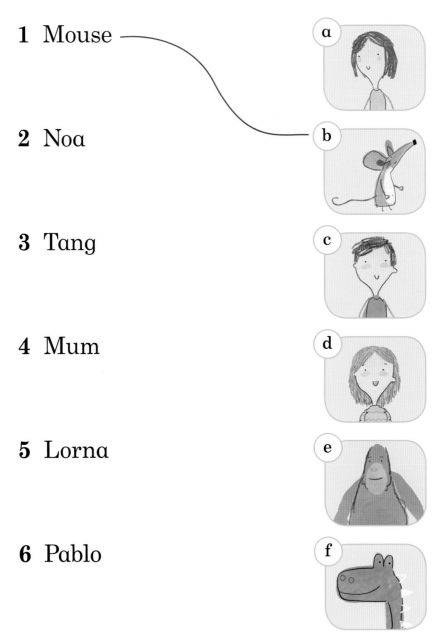

2 Look and read. Put a ✓ or a ✗ in the boxes.

1 This is a television. ✓

2 This is a boy. ☐

3 This is a book. ☐

4 This is a picture. ☐

5 This is a bird. ☐

3 Look at the pictures. Look at the letters. Write the words.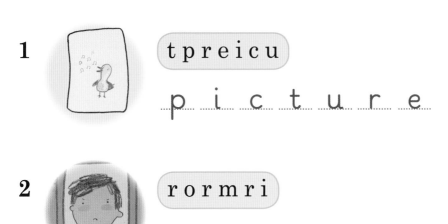

1 **t p r e i c u**

   p i c t u r e

2 **r o r m r i**

   ....

3 **o k b o**

   ....

4 **i b d r**

   ....

5 **e c f a**

   ....

Look and read. Write *yes* or *no*.

1 The bird is yellow. ....yes....

2 Pablo is under the tree. ....

3 The mirror is black. ....

4 Tang is sad. ....

5 There are six animals. ....

5 **Find the words.**

think
picture
mirror
book

a d t t h i n k e t s p o l p i c t u r e f j y m i r r o r x e p s t b o o k r h w y

6 Write the missing letters.

oo   rr   pp   ee   oo

1  f o o t

2  t r ....

3  h a .... y

4  b .... k

5 m i .... o r

7 Listen and color.
Use the colors below. 🎧 ⬡

8 Find the words. 📖

e	i	j	h	a	p	p	y
t	p	i	c	t	u	r	e
l	a	t	p	o	n	e	r
s	k	m	i	r	r	o	r
a	b	f	w	i	v	t	h
d	o	a	k	o	h	e	d
e	o	d	e	t	r	e	e
r	k	p	o	i	h	t	y

happy   sad   mirror

book   picture   tree

9 Match the words.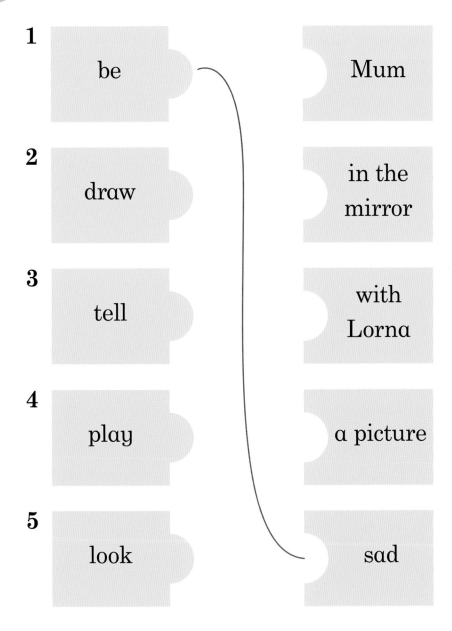

1 be   Mum

2 draw   in the mirror

3 tell   with Lorna

4 play   a picture

5 look   sad

10 **Circle the correct words.**

1 The bird is in the
  a house. **b** tree.

2 Pablo has a
  a picture. **b** book.

3 Pablo is playing with
  a Llama. **b** Lorna.

4 Pablo and Lorna are
  a sad. **b** happy.

11  **Look and read. Write *yes* or *no*.**

1 Mouse draws Pablo.   ...yes...

2 Pablo has yellow hair.   ....

3 Pablo's face is happy.   ....

4 Mouse is gray.   ....

5 Pablo's shirt is green.   ....

12 **Circle the correct sentences.**

1  **a** Pablo's face is happy.

b Pablo's face is sad.

2  **a** Pablo looks in the mirror.

b Pablo looks in the book.

3  **a** Pablo draws Mouse.

b Mouse draws Pablo.

4  **a** Pablo puts a picture in front of his face.

b Pablo puts a book in front of his face.

13 Complete the sentences.
Write a—d.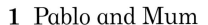

1 Pablo and Mum   <u>b</u>

2 I cannot find

3 I can tell Mum

4 His face is not happy . . .

---

a but Pablo is happy.

b are at home.

c my words.

d with a picture!

14 **Choose the correct words and write them on the lines.**

mirror	book	Pablo
sad	face	Mouse

Pablo looks in the ¹ <u>mirror</u>.

His ² .... is sad. Pablo puts

a ³ .... in front of his face.

"I don't like my ⁴ .... face,"

says ⁵ ....

15 Who says this?

Mum   Pablo   Mouse   Tang

1 "Sorry, Pablo cannot play today,"

says .... Mum ....

2 "Look. Your face is sad,"

says ....

3 "My face is sad, but I'm not sad!"

says ....

4 "Look in the mirror,"

says ....

5 "I'm happy, and my face is happy!"

says ....

16 Put a ✓ by the things you can see.

1	animals	✓	**2**	a house	
3	a girl		**4**	a boy	
5	flowers		**6**	books	
7	a picture		**8**	a mirror	
9	a pencil		**10**	shoes	
11	a tree		**12**	a dog	
13	a television		**14**	a window	

17 **Order the story. Write 1—4.**

.... Pablo draws a picture.
"You *can* play with Lorna!"
says Mum.

....1.... Pablo and Mum are at home.
"Sorry, Pablo cannot play today,"
says Mum.

.... Pablo looks in the mirror. His
face is sad, but he is not sad.

.... Pablo does not understand.
Pablo's face is sad.

18 **Ask and answer the questions with a friend.**

1 What's your name?

My name is . . .

2 Is your face happy or sad?

3 Are you happy or sad?

19 **Sing the song.**

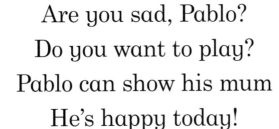

Are you sad, Pablo?
Do you want to play?
Pablo can show his mum
He's happy today!

Pablo's mum wants to know
Does Pablo want to play?
His face is sad.
His mum phones Lorna.
"He can't play today."

Pablo doesn't understand.
He wants to play.
He can't find his words.
He wants to tell his mum,
but what can he say?

Are you sad, Pablo?
Do you want to play?
Pablo can show his mum
He's happy today!

47

Visit www.ladybirdeducation.co.uk
for more FREE Ladybird Readers resources

✓ Digital edition of every title

✓ Audio tracks (US/UK)

✓ Answer keys

✓ Lesson plans

✓ Role-plays

✓ Classroom display material

✓ Flashcards

✓ User guides

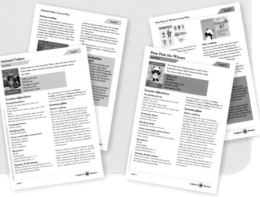

Register and sign up to the newsletter to receive your FREE classroom resource pack!

To access the audio and digital versions of this book:

1 Go to www.ladybirdeducation.co.uk
2 Click "Unlock book"
3 Enter the code below

9dVHmwziLg